P9-CRP-869

THE GOLDEN MEAN

In Which
The Extraordinary Correspondence of
Griffin & Sabine Concludes

Written and Illustrated
by
Nick Bantock

First published in the United States
in 1993 by Chronicle Books.

Printed in China

Bantock, Nick.
The Golden Mean : in which the extraordinary correspondence
of Griffin and Sabine concludes / written and
illustrated by Nick Bantock
p. cm.
ISBN 1-895714-03-6
1. Imaginary letters. 2. Toy and movable books.
I. Title.
PR6052.A54G6 1993
823'.914 C93-091137-7

10 9 8 7 6 5 4 3 2 1

This edition first published in Canada in 1993 by
Raincoast Books, 112 East 3rd Avenue,
Vancouver, B.C. V5T 1C8

To Annie Barrows

CEPHEUS
ZENITH
Schedar
Caph
Gamma
Ruchbah
Mirfak
PERSEUS
Algol
Menkib
Zeta
PAR AVION

SABINE/ AUG 12

I WAS SURE I UNDERSTOOD. YET YOU WERE NOT HERE WHEN I RETURNED & THERE WAS NO SIGN THAT YOU EVER HAD BEEN HERE. I ASKED THE WOMAN NEXT DOOR ABOUT YOU, & SHE LOOKED AT ME AS THOUGH I'D GONE ROUND THE BEND, SAYING SHE'D BEEN IN TWICE TO CHECK THE HOUSE & THERE WAS CERTAINLY NO SIGN OF ANYONE LIVING IN THE PLACE.

I WANDERED AROUND, TRYING TO FIGURE THINGS OUT. THEN I FOUND THE OLD AIR MAIL LABEL YOU SENT ME ON A POSTCARD LAST WINTER, RIGHT AFTER YOU FIRST STARTED STAYING HERE. IT WAS STILL IN THE CUPBOARD.

TODAY COMES YOUR CARD SAYING YOU

GRYPHON CARDS

WERE IN THIS HOUSE FOR SEVEN DAYS AFTER MY RETURN.

I AM BEWILDERED.

I NEED YOU BADLY. GRIFFIN

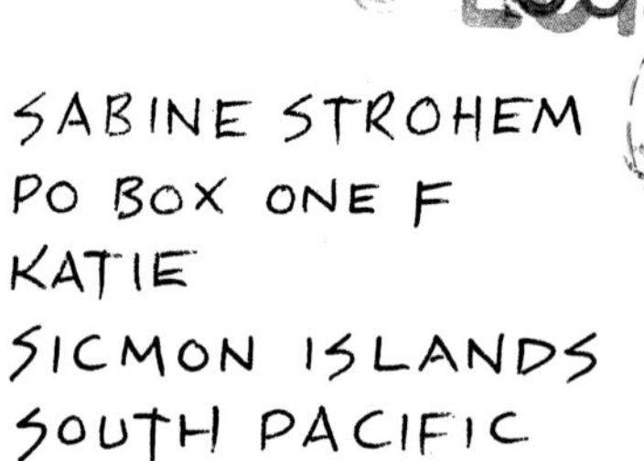

SABINE STROHEM
PO BOX ONE F
KATIE
SICMON ISLANDS
SOUTH PACIFIC

EXPRESS
8+2
KATIN
SICMON
8
ISLANDS
Air M

Griffin – I have always known we were polarized, but I didn't expect this. We have a bigger problem than I thought. The gap is wide.

I'm frustrated at not being able to hold you in my arms; I feel like I'm being teased by an unseen adversary. My consolation comes from being home, where I became myself again once I'd washed my face in the sea and dug my feet into Katie sand.

Do not worry. We will find an answer.

love Sabine

How's Minnaloushe? He wanted to come back with me, but I told him he wouldn't get on with the macaws.

AIR MAIL

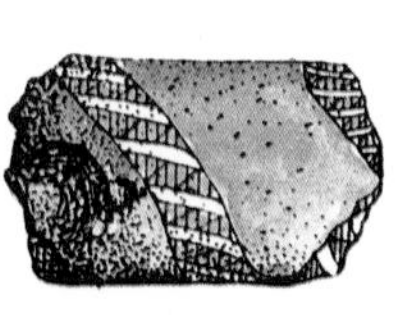

Griffin Moss
41 Yeats Avenue
London NW3
England.

FUN
CITY
MATCHES

SABINE / SEPT 3

MINNALOUSHE HUNG AROUND FOR A FEW DAYS, ACTING AS IF HE'D LOST SOMETHING. NOW HE'S BACK TO HIS WANDERING WAYS.

I TOO AM GETTING MY BALANCE BACK. I TOLD MYSELF THAT THERE ARE NO RULES ANY MORE, THAT I JUST HAVE TO KEEP GOING UNTIL WE FIND OUT WHY THIS IS HAPPENING TO US.

MAYBE I READ TOO MANY SCIENCE FICTION BOOKS WHEN I WAS A KID, BUT THIS OVERLAPPING OF TIME & SPACE SEEMS LIKE WE'RE LIVING IN PARALLEL UNIVERSES. DO YOU THINK WE ARE SEPARATED FOR LIFE, EACH UNABLE TO EXIST IN THE OTHER'S PRESENCE?

ALL MY LOVE
GRIFFIN

GRYPHON CARDS

SABINE STROHEM
PO BOX ONE F
KATIE
SICMON ISLANDS
SOUTH PACIFIC

LIRE 4
SUL BOLLETTINO
POSTALI
LIRE QUATTRO
KATIE 8
2ª LIRE 50
SULLA RICEVUTA
CENT. DIECI
CENT. PACCHI 25 1ª PARTE
SUL BOLLETTINO
POSTALI 2ª LIRE 1
SULLA RICEVUTA
CENT. 25
SULLA RICEVUTA
LIRE DUE

Griffin — I think that the concept of parallel universes is too grand. This, I sense, is more personal — a test of our tenacity. If we solve our problem, we gain the reward of each other.
Since I returned, the islands seem subtly different. I can't explain it, but something is bothering me. I'm having a hard time starting work on the new stamp designs. Probably my eyes lost their innocence in the six months I was in London. Yet I could swear the air is murky. My family remains the same, though — they are so pleased to have me home.
They wanted to know absolutely everything I'd seen and done. I love them. As I do you.

Sabine

Griffin Moss
41 Yeats Avenue
London NW3
England

Air Mail Par
SABINE STROHEM
PO BOX ONE F
KATIE
SICMON IS.
SOUTH PACIFIC
2

SPECIAL DELIVERY

AIR
AVION
AIR MAIL
TA FIN
7
SIOMON
ISLANDS
2B
SIOMON
TA FIN
2B
1C
ceremonial
spinning top
T 1
S 1
R 1
Q 1
K 5
L 5
M 5
P 1
N 1

Griffin – I'm so pleased you have gone to the country and made your peace with Vereker. I felt that resolution was coming, and I am glad for you.

I'm back at work again. The printers made an error on the last Arbah Bc. issue, and the whole lot had to be recalled. It was very odd. They perforated through the heart of the stamp's image. They say they don't know how it happened.

There was another hiccup in paradise — my father broke his ankle playing gumball with the grandchildren. He's a hopeless patient. Mother and I take turns keeping him in his chair. Tell me the banana boat story

Sabine

Griffin Moss
17 Cott Cottages
Dartington
Devon UK

YES. WE HAVE NO BANANAS.

SABINE / OCT 6

SINCE YOU ASKED:
PUCK, THE WELL-KNOWN WIZARD & CHANGER OF THINGS, INCLUDING HIMSELF, HAS HAD HIS WAND STOLEN BY THE DREADED LUGS. PUCK SETS OFF IN PURSUIT, WITH HIS SIDEKICK, FIN. HOWEVER, WITHOUT HIS WAND, HIS SPELLS ONLY HALF-WORK, & HE & FIN END UP AS A SEMI-BANANA-BOAT, HEADING DOWNSTREAM TO RECAPTURE THE WAND.

I HAVEN'T DECIDED WHAT HAPPENS NEXT. TO TELL THE TRUTH, I DON'T KNOW ABOUT THE STORY, BUT I QUITE LIKE THE PICTURES.

THIS KEEPS ME BUSY & REASONABLY SANE DURING THE DAY. AT NIGHT, HOWEVER, I'M TOO RESTLESS TO SLEEP. I PROWL ABOUT THE GARDEN LIKE A LION IN A CAGE.

I MISS YOU
GRIFFIN.

SABINE STROHEM
PO BOX 1 F
KATIE
SICMON ISLANDS
SOUTH PACIFIC

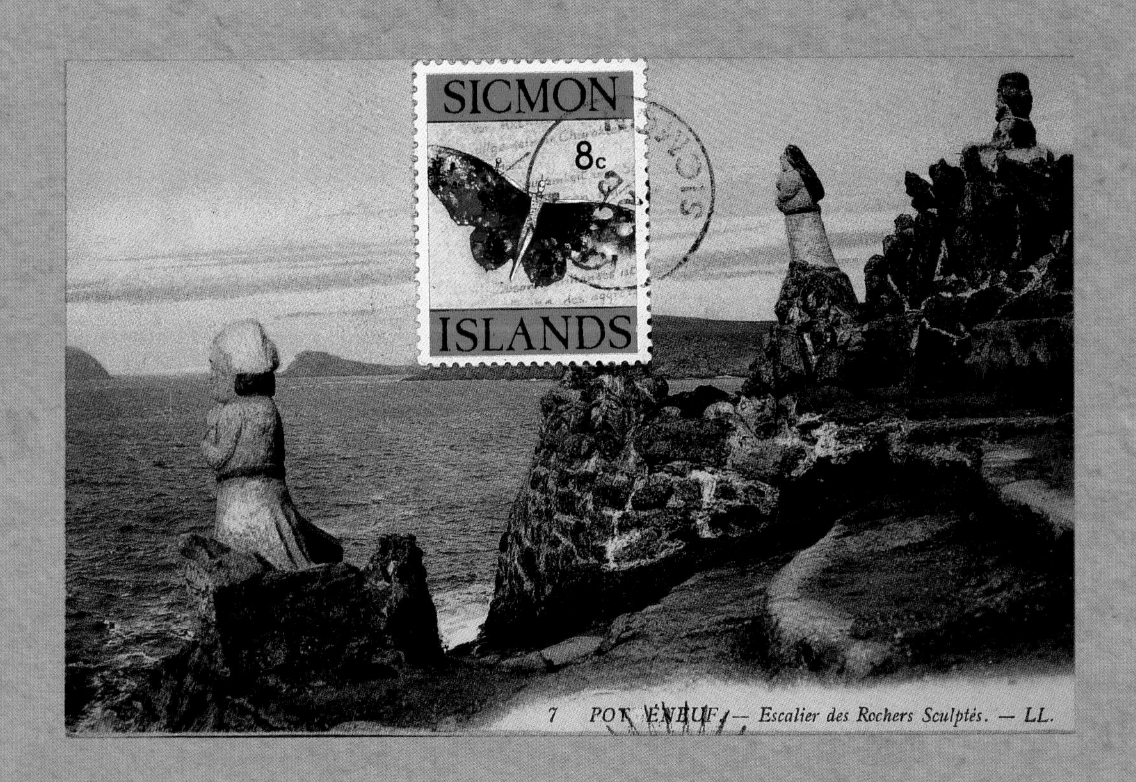
SICMON
8c
ISLANDS
7 POT ENEUF. — Escalier des Rochers Sculptés. — LL.

Mr. Griffin Moss

CARTE POSTALE

Air

Please allow me to introduce myself. My name is Victor Frolatti, and I have recently arrived on the Sicmons where I met a dear young woman called Sabine Strohem. She tells me that you and she are very close. That is charming and to me professionally interesting. Would you mind giving me a few details? Nothing personal, I assure you. Just a little background information about the form of your communication. Dear Sabine has been so helpful, I felt sure you wouldn't mind my humble request. Yours Victor Frolatti

ADRESSE

Mr. Griffin Moss
17 Cott Cottages
Dartington
Devon
England.

As a postcard aficionado you will appreciate this old card from my collection. Unlike you and Sabine, I am no artist, but I enter into the spirit of your liaison.

PAR AVION
via AIR MAIL
JAPAN AIR LINES

SABINE/ OCT 10
WHO'S VICTOR FROLATTI?
I GOT THIS SYCOPHANTIC
CARD FROM SOMEONE OF
THAT NAME SAYING HE KNOWS
YOU AND HE KNOWS ABOUT US. HE
WANTS ME TO TELL HIM ABOUT OUR
RELATIONSHIP.
TO PUT IT MILDLY, THAT'S A VERY
DISTURBING REQUEST FROM A STRANGER.
EXACTLY WHAT DOES HE KNOW ABOUT
YOU AND ME? YOU DIDN'T GIVE HIM MY
ADDRESS, SURELY?
HE CALLS YOU DEAR SABINE —
PATRONIZINE FART!
IT'S WEIRD GETTING A CARD FROM
THE ISLANDS FROM SOMEONE OTHER
THAN YOU. I DON'T LIKE IT.
LOVE GRIFFIN

GRYPHON CARDS

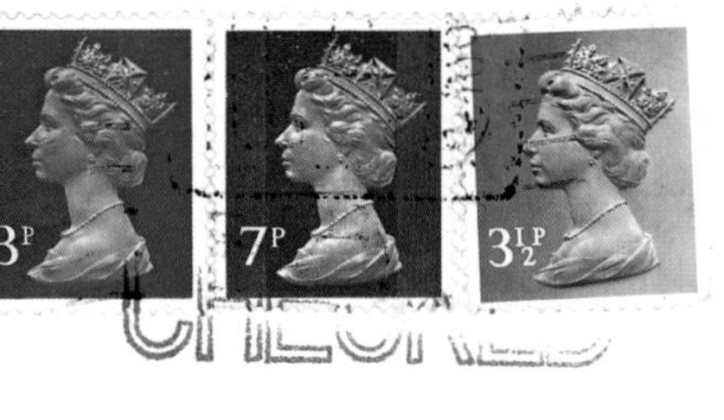

SABINE STROHEM
PO BOX ONE F
KATIE
SICMON ISLANDS
SOUTH PACIFIC

Sfumato

Griffin Moss
17 Cott Cottages
Dartington
Devon England

AIR MAIL

QUEPOL
8

Mr. Griffin Moss

As you didn't reply to my first card I must assume you are reticent to assist me in my investigations. It is critical that you do so.

Miss Strohem's parents confirmed my suspicions that you and she have a fully formed one-way visual telepathy. Do you realize how rare that is? As you may know, I am a scientific journalist frequently published.

In my opinion it is your moral and social obligation to allow the scientific community access to your experiences. Miss Strohem has become stubborn and will not show me your correspondence. I will undoubtedly persuade her in the end, but perhaps you could reason with her.

I feel certain you will comply with my request that you send me her cards and letters to you.

Yours,

Victor Frolatti F.C.P.R.

Carte Postale

Adresse

Mr. Griffin Mo
17 Cott Cottages
Dartington, Dev
England.

SABINE/ OCT 29

IN THE POST THAT FOLLOWED YOUR REASSURING LETTER CAME ANOTHER UNREASSURING CARD FROM FROLATTI. UNLIKE THE FIRST OBSEQUIOUS MISSIVE, THIS ONE HAD AN UNDERTONE OF THREAT. HE WANTS OUR CORRESPONDANCE — WHAT A FUCKING NERVE. WHO DOES HE THINK HE IS? THE SCIENCE POLICE? HE MAY CALL HIMSELF A "SCIENTIFIC JOURNALIST," BUT I THINK HE'S A FREAK HUNTER. YOU AND I, MY LOVE, ARE THE FREAKS.

DO I STILL IGNORE HIM, OR WOULD YOU PREFER ME TO SEND A LETTER TELLING HIM TO GO TO HELL?

ALL MY LOVE GRIFFIN

GRYPHON CARDS

SABINE STROHEM
PO BOX ONE F
KATIE
SICMON ISLANDS
SOUTH PACIFIC

PAR AVION
PER LUCHTPOST
BY AIR MAIL

LIKED YOUR SPINNING TOP SO MUCH, THOUGHT I'D DO ONE OF MY OWN.

The Wheel of Fortune

KATIE 8

Griffin

Do not write to him. It will only provoke him further. He now says he is a psychic analyst and that he wants to write a paper on us. I think he's a despoiler for one of those tabloid newspapers.

I cannot get him to leave me alone, he comes to my house almost daily — I pretend to be out and he waits for me on the porch. Everywhere I turn, he's there, waiting for me.

Something is happening to my vision. When I see you drawing now, it is all out of focus. I must take action. But what do I do? Being apart from you is unbearable.

love Sabine

AIR

Griffin Moss
17 Colt Cottages
Dartington
Devon
England

Mail Par avion
SABINE STROHEM
PO BOX ONE F
KATIE
SICMON ISLANDS
SOUTH PACIFIC

Air M

ARBAH
8
AVION
Griffin Moss
17 Cott Cottages
Dartington
Devon
England

SABINE DEC 12
WE HAVE TO DO SOME-
THING. ANYTHING.
I CANNOT STAND BY AND
WATCH THE DOOR BETWEEN
US CLOSE. WE NEED TO FIND A WAY
TO COME TOGETHER OR BE LOST
TO ONE ANOTHER FOREVER. I'M
NOT CATASTROPHIZING. I KNOW
THIS TO BE TRUE.
IF I CAN'T REACH YOUR WORLD,
AND YOU CAN'T BE IN MINE WHILE
I'M HERE, MAYBE THERE'S ANOTHER
PLACE, HALFWAY. I DON'T KNOW.
I'M RAMBLING.
DON'T THINK OF GIVING IN TO
FROLATTI.
HOLD ON.
I LOVE YOU TOTALLY
GRIFFIN

The Hung Boy

GRYPHON CARDS

A

SABINE STROHEM
PO BOX ONE F
KATIE
SICMON ISLANDS
SOUTH PACIFIC

Air Mail Par avion

SICMON 8+2
AMNESTY WEEK

Griffin

Yes. We've got it. It's so straight forward I could cry – we need to meet on middle ground. I will leave Frolatti in my windwake. The islands will be safer once I'm gone.

Last March in Alexandria, you found a gate that opened onto a different world. Perhaps Alexandria is the place where we could meet. Perhaps the gate will let us both pass through.

Will you meet me there? Will you leave everything behind so that we can be together?

Do not hesitate my love.

I am filled with so much hope.

Sabine

AIR

GRIFFIN MOSS
17 COTT COTTAGES
DARTINGTON
DEVON ENGLAND

The Gordian Mirror

SABINE/ Dec 28

What you suggest is crazy, simplistic and impossible.

But of course I will meet you. There is no reason without you.

I will be at the Pharos in Alexandria on the 21st.

I trust you and I know we shall be together.

Griffin

Bring your angel wings

SABINE STROHEM
PO BOX ONE F
KATIE
SICMON ISLANDS
SOUTH PACIFIC

For some years nothing was heard from either Griffin or Sabine,
until a young doctor in Kenya received an unusual postcard from a stranger.

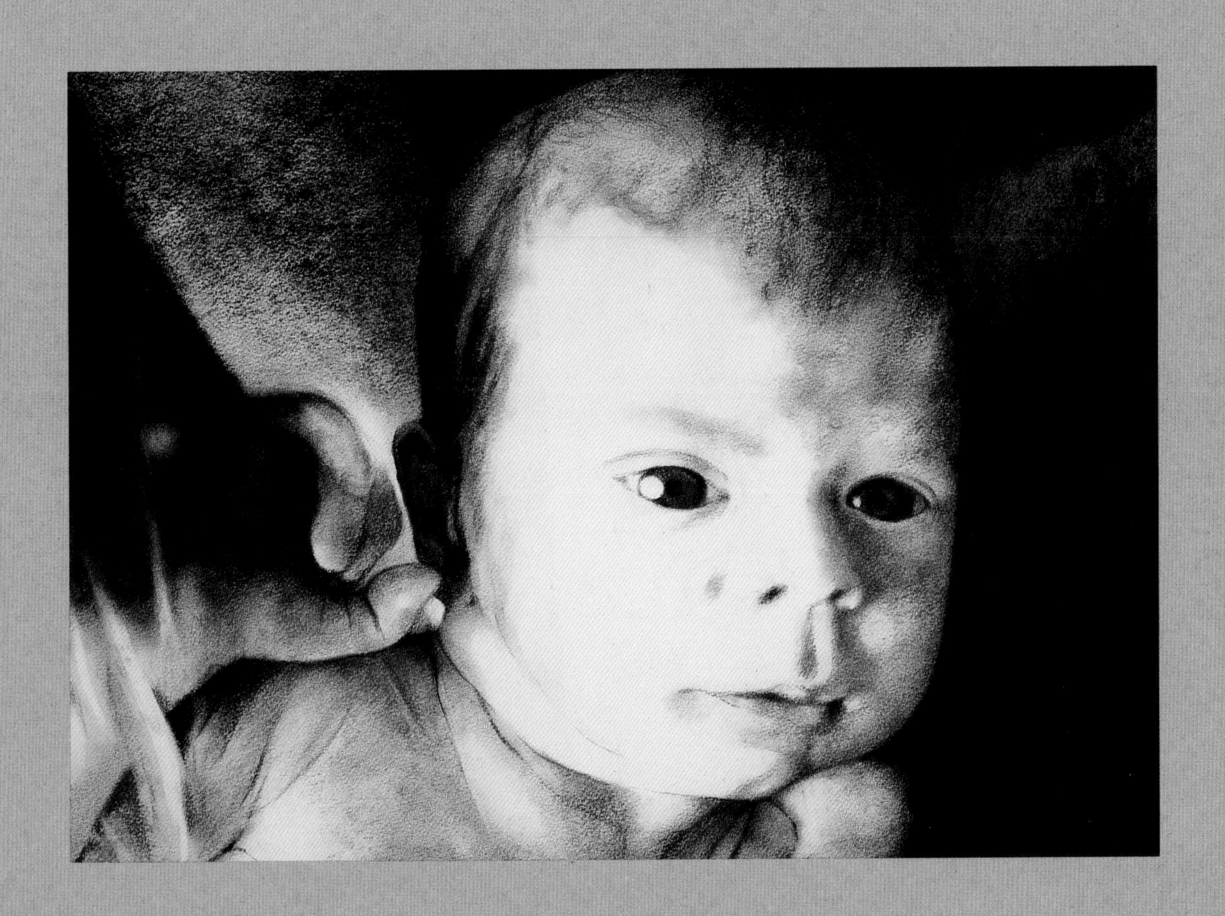

FEB 22

Dear Matthew
It's good to get in touch
with you at last.
We are very impressed with
your general diagnostic abilities.
However we are not convinced
you should be considering
prescribing penicillin for the
Atubi's youngest son.
Write soon – Sabine M. Strohem 39 La Paz pl. San Rosa
Paolo 9T6

Paolo 25f

SPECIAL DELIVERY

DR. MATTHEW SEDON
98 LIVINGSTONE ST.
NAIROBI
KENYA

AIR MAIL

And what rough beast...slouches...to be born .

AIR